stories of
DOGS

Russell Punter

Illustrated by Dusan Pavlic

Reading Consultant: Alison Kelly
Roehampton University

Contents

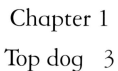

Chapter 1
Top dog   3

Chapter 2
Titch to the rescue   17

Chapter 3
Trouble at Tike's   32

Chapter 1

Top dog

Sprite was on his way to a dog show at the local park.

"I'm sure we'll win first prize," said Sprite's owner, Nick.

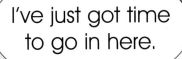

I've just got time to go in here.

Nick went into the pet store next to the park. Sprite waited quietly outside.

"I hope Nick's buying doggy chews," thought Sprite, licking his lips.

Sprite felt a sudden pain. A man had stepped on his paw. He was scruffy and very smelly.

"Out of my way, you pesky pooch," snapped the man. "I can't stand dogs," he added, as he marched away.

When they arrived at the show, Nick put Sprite in an area with lots of other dogs. Sprite introduced himself.

A poodle named Lady sniffed
snootily. "I hope you don't
have fleas," she said to Sprite.
  "Of course not," said Sprite.
"I had a bath this morning."

7

"That won't get you first prize," laughed Lady. "I'm the prettiest, smartest dog here."

The contest is about to start.

Nick took Sprite to get ready. The first round was to find the best looking dog.

One by one, the judges examined the dogs. They stroked their coats...

looked in their ears...

tapped their teeth...

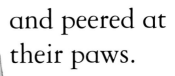

and peered at their paws.

One judge found mud on Sprite's sore paw. She tutted.

"That smelly man made my paw dirty," remembered Sprite.

Tut tut.

The next test was dog control. Sprite followed Nick's commands to sit and stay.

Then Nick called Sprite to his side. But Sprite could only hobble. His paw was too sore to run.

"Ha ha," laughed Lady, as Sprite limped back. "You won't get many marks for that useless performance."

The final test was the
obstacle course. The dogs had
one minute to get around.

Sprite tried. But his sore paw
made him forget his training.

He got
jammed
between the
poles...

fell off the
see-saw...

12

only got
halfway
through the
hoop...

missed the
jump...

and got
trapped under
the net.

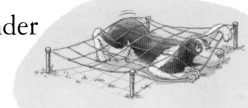

13

"What a disaster," said Sprite.
"I was fastest," boasted Lady.
"The gold cup will be mine."

But as they were about to call
the winner...

Oh no!

"The cup's gone!" cried
a judge.

Dogs and owners looked
shocked. Where was the cup?

Sprite suddenly got a whiff
of a smell he knew. It came
from one of the judges.

"He's not a judge," realized
Sprite. "He's the man who
stepped on my paw."
Sprite grabbed the man's leg.

"Get off!" yelled the man.

He tried to run, but fell over.
With a loud clang, the gold
cup fell out of his coat.

Sprite won first prize for
catching the thief. But even
better, he got a giant
bag of doggy chews
all to himself.

Chapter 2

Titch to the rescue

Titch wanted to be a top sheepdog like Bryn, his dad. Bryn had won lots of medals.

But when Titch tried to round up sheep, things always went wrong.

First, he couldn't get them out of their pen...

then they wouldn't go through the gate in the fence...

18

one sheep
always
managed to
escape...

the others wouldn't
stand still...

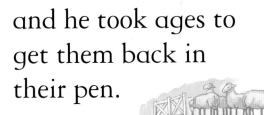

and he took ages to
get them back in
their pen.

One evening, Owen the shepherd took Titch and Bryn for a walk.

"I'll never be as good as you, Dad," woofed Titch sadly.

"You just need to work at it, son," barked Bryn.

Just then, a thick fog began to float around them.

"Quickly boys," said Owen.
He and Bryn ran ahead. Titch
lost sight of them.

Titch heard a shout and a
yelp. His dad and Owen were
in trouble.

Titch ran forward. But
Owen and Bryn had vanished.

Woof! Down
here, son.

Titch heard his dad's voice.
It was coming from a deep,
dark hole in the ground.

Titch could see his dad at the bottom of the hole. Owen lay still on the ground beside him.

"I'll get help," barked Titch. The young dog raced down the hillside through the fog.

"Farmer Ellis lives nearby," thought Titch. "He'll help."

Titch hurtled through the valley. He saw the lights of a farmhouse in the distance.

24

Mr. Ellis was in the
farmyard. Titch rushed up
to him, barking loudly.

"Hello Titch," smiled Mr.
Ellis. "Are you lost, boy?"
He patted Titch and tried to
lead him indoors.

25

Titch pulled away and shook his head towards the hillside.

"I'll take you home tomorrow boy," said Mr. Ellis.

Titch kept barking. "If only humans could understand dog talk," he thought.

Mr. Ellis headed indoors.
"How can I make him follow
me?" wondered Titch.
Then he had an idea.

He ran to Mr. Ellis's sheep
pen. Jumping up, he tugged
at the rope on the pen gate. It
came free and the gate opened.

The sheep ran noisily into the farmyard.

"What are you doing?" cried Mr. Ellis.

Before the farmer could stop him, Titch herded the sheep out of the yard and up the hillside.

Titch tried to remember all his dad's tricks. Keeping the flock together, he steered them along. Mr. Ellis ran behind.

Titch's plan was working. He led the farmer and his sheep to the hole in the ground.

Mr. Ellis heard Bryn's bark and looked down the hole. "So that's what you were up to, Titch," he cried.

Mr. Ellis went for help and Owen and Bryn were rescued from the hole.

A week later, Titch won a medal at last. But it wasn't for shepherding.

Well done, son.

It was for bravery.

Chapter 3

Trouble at Tike's

Mr. Tike couldn't afford to repair his dogs' home. So he was selling the creaking old building, along with his dogs.

The dogs were sad to see Mr. Tike go. He'd rescued them and given them a safe home.

"I wonder who the new owner will be," woofed Bob the collie.

"I hope they'll be as nice as Mr. Tike," yelped Pip the pointer.

33

One day, two strangers arrived at Tike's.

"We want to buy your sweet little doggy home," said Mrs. Hood.

Mr. Tike showed them around.

In the yard, the dogs rushed up to greet the visitors.

"You let the mutts, er, dogs run around?" asked Mr. Wink.

"Of course," replied Mr. Tike. "How charming," said Mrs. Hood, with a sickly smile.

Two days later, the new owners took over.

"Now then," scowled Mrs. Hood as soon as Mr. Tike had gone. "Let's get these hairy fleabags out of the way."

The dogs were rounded up.
They yelped and barked as
they were locked in a cage.

Now we can get to work.

"What's going on?" Heidi the
dachshund asked the others.
"Mr. Tike never treated us like
this," said Winnie the bulldog.

"We must get out," said Pip.
"Let me try,"
said Heidi.
She took
a deep
breath and
squeezed
out of the
cage.

"Grab the
keys!" cried Bob.
Heidi climbed
onto a kennel
and jumped up
to the keys.

38

Heidi freed the others and they ran into the house. A scrapbook was on the table.

"Hood and Wink are bank robbers," gasped Bob.

Just then, the dogs heard voices and ran into the yard. "Remember when this was just a field?" said Mrs. Hood.

"It was a great place to bury our gold, until we could escape from jail."

40

"If only they hadn't built this stinking dog house on top," moaned Mr. Wink.

"We'll bulldoze it to dig up the loot," he added, "after we've dumped those mutts. Hey, where are they?"

41

The dogs had heard enough. Winnie leapt onto Mr. Wink's head...

Pip bit him on the bottom...

Ooww!

and Heidi tugged on his leg.

Tina the terrier grabbed
Mrs. Hood's necklace...

Aagh!

Bob sank his
teeth into
her jacket...

and the
Pekingese
twins nipped
her ankles.

43

Dot the Dalmatian fired
chunky dog food into the
crooks' faces.

Take that!

SPLAT!
SPLURGE!

"Run for it!" cried Mr. Wink.
The dogs chased the pair out
of the home and down the road.

The yummy smell of *Meaty Chunks* soon had every dog in town on the crooks' trail.

Bob and the other hounds chased the crooks to the local police station.

The police decided to give the reward money for catching Hood and Wink to Mr. Tike. He promptly bulldozed his old dogs' home...

...and built a brand new one.

Tike's Luxury
Dogs' Home

Series editor:
Lesley Sims

First published in 2007 by Usborne Publishing Ltd., Usborne House,
83-85 Saffron Hill, London EC1N 8RT, England. www.usborne.com
Copyright © 2007 Usborne Publishing Ltd.

48